OTHER YEARLING BOOKS YOU WILL ENJOY:

Headlines, MALCOLM HALL

A Toad for Tuesday, RUSSELL E. ERICKSON

Maybe, A Mole, JULIA CUNNINGHAM

Harry Cat's Pet Puppy, GEORGE SELDEN

The Times They Used To Be, LUCILLE CLIFTON

Miss Clafooty and the Demon, J. DAVID TOWNSEND

The Strange Story of the Frog Who Became a Prince, ELINOR LANDER HORWITZ

Morris Brookside, A Dog, MARJORIE WEINMAN SHARMAT

The Visitor, GENE SMITH

The Carp in the Bathtub, BARBARA COHEN

Three Friends

by

ROBERT FREMLIN

Illustrated by

WALLACE TRIPP

A Yearling Book

To Carol

Published by
Dell Publishing Co., Inc.
1 Dag Hammarskjold Plaza
New York, New York 10017

Text Copyright © 1975 by Robert Fremlin
Illustrations Copyright © 1975 by Wallace Tripp

Yearling ® TM 913705, Dell Publishing Co., Inc.

ISBN: 0-440-48699-8
Reprinted by arrangement with Little, Brown and Company, Inc.
Printed in the United States of America
Sixth Dell Printing—August 1978

Pig Disappears

SQUIRREL HURRIED along the road to Pig's pen.

"What can be wrong now?" he worried. "I knew something would happen. If it isn't one trouble it's another."

Cat was waiting in front of Pig's pen. Cat looked cross.

"Cat," shouted Squirrel, "I got your mes-
sage and came as fast as I could. What is the
matter?"

"Pfah," said Cat. "Pig is the matter. Look
at that."

Cat pointed to a sign on Pig's door.

"What? Pig selling his pen? Why would Pig do such a thing?"

Cat frowned. "Pig has disappeared. Apparently run away. Typical Pig-like stunt if I ever heard of one. He left this note in my mailbox, and I've just come to see if it's true."

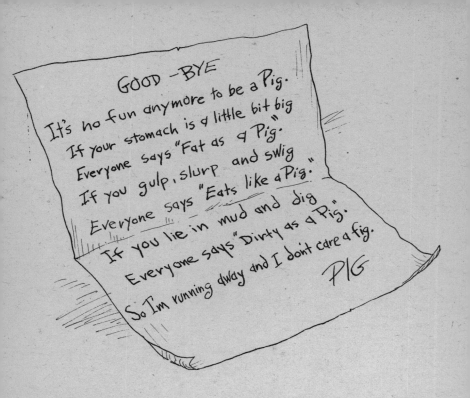

GOOD -BYE

It's no fun anymore to be a Pig.
If your stomach is a little bit big
Everyone says "Fat as a Pig."
If you gulp, slurp and swig
Everyone says "Eats like a Pig."
If you lie in mud and dig
Everyone says "Dirty as a Pig."
So I'm running away and I don't care a fig.

PIG

"Oh Cat, this is terrible news," said Squirrel.

"It's not very good poetry either," grumbled Cat, looking at the note.

"I thought Pig liked being a pig."

8

"Maybe today is just a bad day for being a pig," replied Cat.

"Poor Pig," said Squirrel. "Where can he have gone?"

Suddenly there was a crash from inside Pig's pen. Squirrel jumped behind Cat.

"I think we had better see what that noise is all about," whispered Cat. "Don't be afraid, Squirrel."

Cat and Squirrel slowly pushed open the door and went inside.

They found Pig in the kitchen, stuffing food into a suitcase on the floor.

"Pfah!" said Cat. "In the kitchen. I might have known."

"Not for long," said Pig. "I'm on my way as soon as I finish packing. Squirrel, will you hand me that big bag of jellybeans?"

"But why are you running away?" asked Squirrel.

"Because nobody wants a pig around, that's why," said Pig. "Yesterday at the picnic everyone was mad at me because I ate all the cake. And Rabbit won't let me come to dinner again just because I helped myself to all the lettuce and fell into the pie. And even you, Cat, told me I have bad manners."

"I did *not* say that," said Cat. "I said you eat like a pig."

"Oh it's no use," said Pig. "I'm going. Can you reach that big jar of pickles, Cat?"

Pig, Cat and Squirrel crowded around the suitcase.

"Let me see," said Pig, "I've got the butterscotch pudding, catsup, chocolate-covered doughnuts, candy bars . . ."

"There are no clothes in that suitcase," said Cat.

". . . peanut butter, mustard, marshmallows," counted Pig.

"But Pig, we don't *want* you to run away," said Squirrel.

"I'm almost gone," said Pig. "Practically out the door, in fact."

"What is in that bag on the table?" asked Cat.

"My lunch, of course," said Pig.

"Pfah," said Cat.

Pig tried to shut the suitcase. It would not close. He stood on it. The suitcase still would not close.

"Cat, Squirrel, will you help me?"

Pig, Cat and Squirrel stood on the suitcase.

They jumped on it. They danced on it. But
the suitcase would not close.

"It must be a broken suitcase," said Pig.

"It must be that big jar of pickles," said Cat.

"Hurray," said Squirrel. "If you cannot close your suitcase you cannot run away."

"Humph," said Cat. "If you take something out you can close your suitcase."

"But I cannot take out food," said Pig.

They looked at the suitcase on the floor. Butterscotch pudding was leaking out the side.

"Poor me," groaned Pig. "I thought if I ran away I could be different. Now I feel miserable."

"But Pig," said Squirrel, "we like you just as you are."

"Besides, there's really nothing wrong with being a pig," said Cat.

Pig looked at his two friends. "I suppose if I *must* be a pig I would rather be a pig here than anywhere else," he sighed.

"Then you'll stay?" asked Squirrel. "Good. Why don't we unpack everything and have a party?"

"A not-going-away party," said Cat.

"Well, I *am* a bit hungry," said Pig.

So they emptied Pig's suitcase on the kitchen table. Then they all had a fine dinner.

The Circus

IN THE WEEDS behind Pig's pen stood two paper tents and a cardboard box. Pig and his friends were having their circus. Squirrel began to cut a hole in the box.

"What are you doing, Squirrel?" asked Cat.

"I'm finishing my cage. I am the tiger this year."

Squirrel climbed into the box and peeked out the hole.

"Cat, I *do* look like a fierce tiger in a cage, don't I?"

"Humph," said Cat. "You look like a squirrel in a cardboard box."

"You just wait until Pig paints my stripes," said Squirrel. "Then I will look like a tiger."

"Do you have to sit in that box all day?"
asked Cat.

"Only until lunch," said Squirrel. "After
lunch Sparrow is the tiger."

"Well, what is Sparrow this morning?"

"The giraffe," said Squirrel. "He is over
there next to the merry-go-round."

"I don't see a merry-go-round," said Cat.
"I see Dog and Donkey tied to a stick."

"But that is the merry-go-round," said
Squirrel softly. "Anyway, *Pig* said it was."

"Pfah," said Cat.

Just then Pig himself came over the hill and hurried toward them carrying a box.

"Why is Pig dressed in that tablecloth?" asked Cat.

"That's his cape," said Squirrel. "Pig is the magician."

"Cat, Squirrel, come see my magic show," said Pig. He led them to one of the tents.

"Sit in front so you won't miss anything," said Pig. "Hurry, before the crowd comes."

Pig opened his magic box and dumped out a can of baking powder, a paper mustache and a clothesline. He pasted the mustache under his nose and stepped onto the box. Cat and Squirrel waited for Pig's magic show to begin.

Pig practiced a few waves with his magic wand. "The crowd will be here any minute," he said. "Then I will start."

Pig waited on his box. Cat and Squirrel waited on their chairs.

They waited and waited. But no one came.

"Pig, you can begin," said Squirrel. "Cat and I will pretend we are a crowd."

"Ladies and gentlemen," Pig announced to Cat and Squirrel, "first, I shall make a key disappear with this magic powder."

Squirrel clapped loudly. Cat yawned.

Pig took a key out of his pocket and sprinkled baking powder on it. Then he blew on the powder.

"Poof!"

Some of the powder blew into Pig's nose.

"Ahh-choo!"

Pig fell off his magic box. He sat up and looked around.

"Where is it?" he asked.

"Where is what?" asked Squirrel.

"The key," said Pig. "Where is the key?"

"You made it disappear," said Squirrel. "That was a very good trick, Pig."

"Don't be silly," said Pig. "I did not make the key disappear. I lost it."

Pig, Cat and Squirrel looked in the grass but could not find the key.

"Let's go, Squirrel," said Cat. "I want to ride the merry-go-round."

"Wait," said Pig. "I have a much better trick. Here, tie me with this magic rope and I will escape in a few seconds. You should stay. You'll be sorry if you miss this good trick."

Squirrel looked at Cat.

"Oh, all right," muttered Cat.

He and Squirrel tied the clothesline around Pig.

"No, there should be more knots," said
Pig.

"But Pig," said Squirrel, "you will never
untie these knots."

"Nonsense," said Pig. "These knots are
too simple. You must tie more knots or it
won't be any fun to escape."

Cat and Squirrel wound more rope around
Pig.

"Tighter," said Pig. "Tie those knots tighter, and don't forget my tail. You must tie my tail, too."

When they finished, Pig looked like a ball of rope with two ears sticking out.

"Now," said Pig from inside the ball, "are you ready?"

"We are ready," said Cat and Squirrel.

"Then here I come!" shouted Pig.

Nothing happened.

"Here — I — come," said Pig.

"Keep trying, Pig," cried Squirrel.

"Ridiculous," yawned Cat.

"I will escape now," said Pig.

Nothing happened. Pig grunted inside the ball.

Cat and Squirrel waited and waited.

Suddenly the ball of rope fell to the ground and began to roll back and forth.

"Help! Help!" squeaked Pig. "Get me out of here!"

Cat and Squirrel untied Pig.

"There was something wrong with those knots," said Pig.

"Humph," said Cat. "Let's go, Squirrel. There is no magic in this show."

"No, wait!" yelled Pig. "You haven't seen anything yet. The next trick is the best of all."

Pig stepped on his magic box again.

"I will change a dozen eggs into chickens. Now, watch carefully."

Pig stuffed his pockets full of eggs.

"I will tap the eggs with my magic wand and change them into chickens."

Pig tapped the wand against a pocket.

"Crack!"

"Oh no," said Squirrel. "I do not like the sound of that sound."

Pig tapped another pocket.
"Squish!"

"That is no chicken," said Cat. "Chickens
do not say 'squish.'"

"I will now turn around three times to make the magic work."

Pig hopped in a circle. His pants crunched as he turned.

"Now I will show you what I have in my pockets," said Pig.

Cat frowned. "I think I can guess," he said.

Pig reached into a pocket. He reached into another pocket. His smile disappeared. His face got very red.

"The magic is turning Pig yellow!" shouted Squirrel.

Pig's pants were covered with yellow goo.

Pig took his hooves out of his pockets. His hooves were yellow, too.

"Ladies and gentlemen," Pig said very quietly to Cat and Squirrel, "this magic show is all over."

"Humph," grumbled Cat. "That egg is all over."

Pig slowly stepped down from his magic box. He was yellow and sticky.

"I must go home now and change my clothes," he said glumly.

Pig, Cat and Squirrel started across the field toward Pig's pen.

"Poor me," said Pig. "I was foolish to be a magician. Now I am all yellow and sticky. I should have been the elephant. They did ask me to be the elephant, you know."

"You would have been a very good elephant," said Squirrel.

"Perfect size," sniffed Cat.

At last they came to Pig's pen.

"Now I can change these sticky clothes,"
said Pig. "Then we will have cookies and
lemonade."

Pig reached into his pocket.

"Oh, that horrible magic set!" he shouted.

"What is wrong?" asked Squirrel.

"The key that disappeared. It was the key to my pen!"

Cat looked at Squirrel and sighed. Then they boosted sticky Pig through a window. And after Pig changed his clothes, the three friends made a bag of cookies disappear.

New Suit for Squirrel

PIG RESTED on a pillow under his cherry
tree, thinking about pies. His daydream was
suddenly interrupted by an anxious voice. It
was Squirrel, muttering to himself as he hurried along the road.

"Squirrel," called Pig lazily, "come and

talk to me. It's more fun than talking to yourself."

"I cannot stop now, Pig. I am in a big hurry. I am going to buy a new suit."

"A new suit? Squirrel, you don't need a new suit. New suits are just a lot of trouble. They are no good for mud or climbing. And worst of all, you must be very careful with chocolate and jelly."

"But Pig, Cousin Woodchuck is getting married, and I need a new suit for the wedding."

"Oh, weddings are different," said Pig. "You do need a new suit."

"But I'm worried," said Squirrel. "Won't a new suit be expensive?"

"Where are you going to buy it?" asked Pig.

"I heard about a place on Seaville Road . . ."

"What?" interrupted Pig. "Are you crazy, Squirrel? Listen, I know where you can get a new suit for half the price those robbers on Seaville Road will charge you."

"But are they good suits?" asked Squirrel.

"Squirrel, would I recommend this place if the suits were not good?"

Squirrel did not answer.

"Look," said Pig. "They are tremendous suits. You will never find suits like them anywhere else. Come on, Squirrel, I'll take you there."

They hurried into town and Pig led Squirrel to a narrow street down by the river. They stopped in front of a store with a sign that said:

"Now Squirrel, I know all about suits, so let *me* do the talking."

Ferret's store was once a greenhouse. The walls, ceilings and doors were made of glass. Ferret had changed it into a store by putting cardboard over the glass. Wherever Ferret wanted a window, he had not put cardboard.

"Do all new-suit stores look like this?" asked Squirrel.

"Only the very best," Pig answered proudly.

Ferret had been watching them from the
doorway. He stepped out and bowed.

"Good day, gentlemen. Please come this
way. Follow me." He put a paw on Squirrel's
head and an arm around Pig, and steered them
inside.

"At your service, gentlemen," Ferret said, pushing his nose close to Pig. "What service may I have the honor of doing for you?"

"We need a new suit for a wedding," said Pig. "Can you help us?"

"Ah," said Ferret, bowing. "You are interested in one of my artistic creations. I would be most happy to oblige. You wish something distinguished, of course."

"What does 'distinguished' mean?" Squirrel whispered in Pig's ear.

"It means a suit with pockets," whispered Pig.

"Gentlemen," said Ferret, "you have come to the right place. My suits are famous. I once made a suit for Sir Baskerville Hound. You have heard of him, of course."

Pig and Squirrel had not.

"Of course," said Pig.

"We need the suit in a couple of days," said Pig. "Is that possible?"

"You may rest assured that it is possible, sir. Common tailors take weeks to make a suit but I can create a masterpiece in the wink of an eye. Simply a cut of the cloth, a stitch or two, and there you are."

"And, gentlemen," continued Ferret, grinning slyly, "you can choose any cloth from my collection of the most beautiful fabrics in the world."

Ferret pointed at a pile of material thrown on the floor.

"How about this?" asked Squirrel, picking up a dark piece of fabric.

Ferret bowed and shook his head. "Sir, if I may say so, black would be appropriate for a funeral but surely not for a wedding. May I suggest something with a trifle more color — more life?"

"Good idea," said Pig. "Stand back, Squirrel. I can choose better than you."

Pig and Ferret burrowed through the pile.

Finally, Pig chose a shiny fabric with large purple stripes and red squares.

"Oh no!" said Squirrel. "That is *much* too bright. Something darker would be better."

Ferret smiled and wrapped the fabric around Pig.

"If you please, sir, behold. It is not too

bright. And, after all, I am an artist. Can I
not create from this purple and red the quiet-
est, most distinguished suit you ever saw?"

"Can you?" asked Squirrel anxiously.

Ferret's nose twitched. He glanced down quickly at Squirrel.

"Why can't I?" he asked.

"He's right," said Pig, pushing in front of Squirrel. "Why can't he?"

That settled it. Pig smiled and started to leave.

"But wait," said Squirrel from behind Pig. "Aren't you going to take any measurements?"

Ferret bowed to Pig. "No need for that, sir. The suit you gentlemen have ordered will be superb. To an artist inches are mere details. Common tailors measure suits but an artist can create a suit from nothing. And, after all, I am . . ."

"... an artist," finished Pig. "Yes, I under-
stand perfectly."

"Pig," whispered Squirrel, "I still
think ..."

"Squirrel," whispered Pig, "I told you to leave everything to me."

Pig walked out and Squirrel hurried after him. They left Ferret at the doorway, bowing and waving.

"Pig, I'm worried," said Squirrel as they started home. "What if I don't like my new suit?"

"Oh Squirrel, of course you will like it. Didn't I tell Ferret exactly what you want? It's lucky for you I know all about new suits. Nothing can possibly go wrong."

The next day Cat, Pig and Squirrel were at Pig's pen playing a game of rummy.

The doorbell rang. Cat frowned and grumbled over his cards while Pig went to the door.

"Look, Squirrel," said Pig. "Here is a box from Ferret. It must be your new suit."

Cat and Pig crowded around while Squirrel opened the box.

"Oh no!" cried Squirrel. "This cannot be my suit."

"Of course that cannot be your suit," said Cat. "It has big purple stripes, red squares, padded shoulders and seams that do not match."

"It is your suit," said Pig.

"But, Pig, you promised it would be a distinguished suit," said Squirrel.

"It is a very distinguished suit," said Pig.
"It has pockets *and* puffed sleeves."

Cat held up the suit. "What are all those
holes in the jacket?" he asked.

"They are buttonholes, of course," said Pig.

"Pfah," said Cat. "There are no buttons on this jacket."

"It doesn't need buttons," said Pig. "It has a zipper instead."

"Oh, this is terrible," said Squirrel. "I cannot wear that suit to Cousin Woodchuck's wedding."

"Squirrel, you cannot wear that suit *anywhere*," said Cat.

"Oh, you can wear that suit *everywhere*," said Pig. "The ruffles and fringes match your tail perfectly."

Squirrel looked at the suit again. His tail drooped and he began very quietly to sniffle.

"Just a minute," said Cat. "Have you no-
ticed what an odd shape this suit has?"

"There is nothing odd about the shape,"
said Pig, smiling. "Actually, it is the best
shape a suit can have. It's the newest fashion."

Cat frowned. "This is very strange. It looks like this suit was made for a — hmmmm."

Cat looked at the shape of the suit. Then he looked at the shape of Pig.

"Pig, I know where I have seen such an odd shape," said Cat.

Pig stopped smiling. "What do you mean?"

"This suit has a Piggish waist," said Cat.

Cat held the suit against Pig. The suit had a perfect Piggish shape.

"No!!" cried Pig. "It isn't! It can't be!"

"Pig, it is," said Cat. "Look at this card in the box."

FERRET'S FINE FABRICS

New Suit for Pig
Much Obliged
Ferret

That afternoon Cat took Squirrel to Seaville Road to buy a fine new suit for Cousin Woodchuck's wedding. Pig did not go with them. He was busy with his hammer and saw in the weeds behind his pen. When he finished, a new scarecrow stood in the field. The scarecrow had large purple stripes, red squares and a perfect Piggish shape.